Kyle and Kendra
Kindergarten

LATHERS ELEMENTARY

WELCOME STUDENTS
WE ALL LOVE LEARNING!

By Alexander McNeece and Wendy Betway
Illustrated by Jeff Covieo

Ferne Press

Kyle and Kendra Go to Kindergarten

Copyright © 2011 by Alexander McNeece and Wendy Betway
Illustrated by Jeff Covieo
Illustrations created with digital graphics

Printed in the United States of America

Summary: Twin five-year-olds Kyle and Kendra practice letters, numbers, shapes, and colors in preparation for kindergarten.

Library of Congress Cataloging-in-Publication Data
McNeece, Alexander and Betway, Wendy
Kyle and Kendra Go to Kindergarten/Alexander McNeece and Wendy Betway – First Edition
ISBN-13: 978-1-933916-85-9
1. Kindergarten. 2. Elementary school. 3. School readiness.
I. Alexander McNeece and Wendy Betway II. Kyle and Kendra Go to Kindergarten
Library of Congress Control Number: 2011923031

FERNE PRESS

Ferne Press is an imprint of Nelson Publishing & Marketing
366 Welch Road, Northville, MI 48167
www.nelsonpublishingandmarketing.com
(248) 735-0418

Dedication

This book is dedicated to Christie Bronson and kindergarten teachers everywhere who begin the journey of education with much care and love for their students.

Acknowledgments

Special thanks to Kris Yankee, our editor, for her expertise in developing this story.

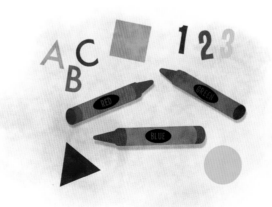

"Momma! It's my birthday," Kyle said.

"I'm five, and now I can go to kindergarten."

"Happy birthday! Are you ready for school?" Mom asked.

"I am. We've practiced all summer. Can Grandma help me some more today?"
Mom replied, "I'm sure she will."

"Daddy, I'm finally five!" Kendra said.
"What a big girl you are. You know what happens now, right?" Dad asked.
"I get to go to Lathers Elementary School, my school."
"That's right, honey."

"Let's see, do you know all of your numbers?" asked Dad.
"We do. Listen," the kids said together, and they counted
to twenty.
"Great job. I'm so proud of you both."

"Happy birthday, kids."

"Grandma, can we go to the playground today?" Kyle asked. "Can we practice our letters?"

"Sure. We can have a birthday snack there and practice anything you want," Grandma replied.

On their way to the playground, Grandma asked, "Do you know all of your letters?"

"We sure do," Kyle and Kendra said together. They sang the ABC song.

♪ ABCD EFG HIJK LMNOP QRS TUV WX Y and Z.
Now I know my ABC's.
Next time won't you sing with me? ♪

LATHERS ELEMENTARY
WELCOME STUDENTS
WE ALL LOVE LEARNING!

"Very good. You are ready," Grandma said.

At the playground, Kendra pulled out a book from Grandma's bag. "I know that a letter can be big or little," Kendra said.
"Big or little?" Kyle asked.

"Sure. Like this. See? A big letter E. And a little letter E looks like this. See?" Kendra replied.

Bb Cc
Dd Ee Ff
Gg Hh Ii
Jj Kk Ll

Mm Nn Oo
Pp Qq Rr Ss
Tt Uu Vv Ww
Xx Yy Zz

"Big letters of the alphabet are called capitals. Letters have sounds too," Grandma said. "Listen, a-a-apple, b-b-banana. Do you know other sounds?"

"D-d-duck," Kendra said.

"F-f-fan," Kyle said.

"G-g-great!" Grandma replied.

"Do you want to play 'color spy'? I spy yellow,"
Grandma said.
Kendra asked, "Is it the big yellow slide?"
"Right. I spy silver," Grandma said.
"I see it!" Kyle shouted.

A plane zoomed through the sky. Kyle imagined soaring through the blue sky and puffy white clouds.

At home, Kyle said, "I spy a circle!"
"Our clock," Grandma replied.
"How about a rectangle?" Kendra asked.
"Our family picture."

Kendra got the toolkit, which held paper and a box of crayons. She drew a shape. "What's this?"
"A triangle," Kyle said. "Can I please share the toolkit?"
"Sure," Kendra replied.
"Thank you."

"We practiced colors, shapes, and letters," Kendra told their parents that evening.
"You're so smart," Dad said. "Now, let's celebrate your birthday."

"Please clean up your toolkit and put it away," Mom said.
"Then can we sing 'Happy Birthday'?" the children asked.

♪♪ **Happy Birthday to you!** ♪♪

After cake, they walked to Lathers Elementary School.
"Kindergarten is so much fun," Dad said.
"What if I forget my numbers, or shapes, or colors, or letters?" Kyle asked.

"The teacher will help you.
You'll learn lots of new things,
too," Mom replied.

The children started to run.

"Please walk in the parking lot," Dad said.

"WOW! Look at all the fun waiting for us," both kids said.

"I can't wait to go to Lathers Elementary School!" Kyle shouted.

"Me, too." Kendra agreed.

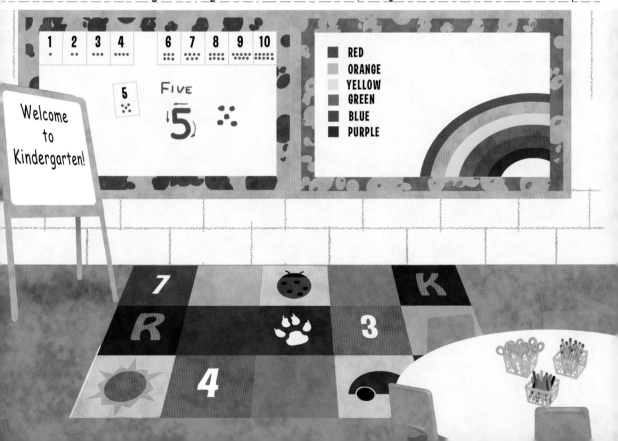

Here are some fun activities for the family!

NAME THESE COLORS:

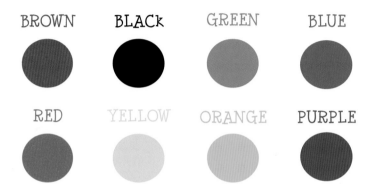

COUNT TO TWENTY:

1, 2, 3, 4, 5, 6, 7, 8, 9, 10, 11, 12, 13, 14, 15, 16, 17, 18, 19, 20

PRINT YOUR FIRST AND LAST NAME ON A PIECE OF PAPER.

DRAW A PICTURE OF YOURSELF WITH CRAYONS AND PENCILS

NAME THESE SHAPES:

DO YOU KNOW THESE PUNCTUATION MARKS? LOOK THROUGH
THE STORY AND FIND WHERE THEY ARE IN EACH SENTENCE

, IS A COMMA.

! IS AN EXCLAMATION POINT.

• IS A PERIOD.

? IS A QUESTION MARK.

" " ARE QUOTATION MARKS.

CUT LETTERS OUT OF A NEWSPAPER OR MAGAZINE
WITH SCISSORS AND MAKE THE ALPHABET

PARENTS: HAVE YOUR CHILD POINT OUT THE FOLLOWING:
- FRONT OF THE BOOK
- BACK OF THE BOOK
- TITLE
- TEXT

Parents,

As an elementary school principal, I can't stress enough how important your role as a parent is to your child's education. You truly are your child's first teacher. Helping prepare your child for kindergarten is one of the most essential tasks you will do. This book was written to help demonstrate some of the simple yet effective things you can do that will have a dramatic impact on your child's kindergarten readiness. In this book, we tried to pack most of the essential skills needed for the first day of school.

Please accept my challenge to read this book to your child, a lot! Actively read and engage with them by singing the alphabet, practicing their letter sounds, pointing out shapes or colors, or even reciting numbers. Also, do the quiz pages each time you read the book. Those pages are very close to one of the first tests your child will take in the fall.

Thank you for your time and dedication to making sure your child is ready for kindergarten, and also for letting this book serve as a resource for you and your child. Kindergarten is the first step that your child takes on their educational journey. We can all agree on the importance of getting a great start. The results of you reading this book, and many more, to them will put your child on the path for success!

Alexander McNeece

About the Authors:

Alexander McNeece received a bachelor's and master's degree in education from Michigan State University. After teaching English for eight years in Southfield, he now works as an administrator in Garden City, Michigan. He speaks both locally and nationally about his books, as well as English Language Arts, and educating at-risk readers. His first book, *Sam Iver: Imminent Threat*, was written for reluctant, video-game-addicted teenage audiences. Please visit his website, www.alexandermcneece.com, for more information. He lives with his wife and two children in Southeastern Michigan.

Wendy Betway has been teaching in Garden City since 1979. She spent several years working with autistic children at the Burger Center before joining the Douglas Elementary staff. At Douglas Elementary, Wendy has taught second, third, and fourth grade as well as music. She shares her love of writing with her students. Writing this book has been a long-time goal of hers, and she is currently working on her second book.

About the Illustrator:

Jeff Covieo has been drawing since he could hold a pencil and hasn't stopped since. He has a BFA in photography from the Center for Creative Studies in Michigan and works in the commercial photography field, though drawing and illustration have been his avocation for years. Other titles illustrated by Jeff include *Cuddling is Like Chocolate, Read to Me, Daddy! My First Football Book,* and *The Ride of Your Life: Fighting Cancer with Attitude.*

If you enjoyed this book, you may enjoy the following books which can be found at your local library:

Goodnight, Moon by Margaret Wise Brown
Mike Mulligan and His Steam Shovel by Virginia Lee Burton
The Very Hungry Caterpillar by Eric Carle
Corduroy by Don Freeman
Bread and Jam for Frances by Russell Hoban
The Carrot Seed by Ruth Krauss
Over in the Meadow by John Langstaff
Chicka Chicka Boom Boom by Bill Martin
Have You Filled a Bucket Today? by Carol McCloud
If You Give a Mouse a Cookie by Laura Numeroff
Good Night, Gorilla by Peggy Rathmann
Oh No! Ah Yes! by Kalli K. Reid
Curious George by H. A. Rey
We're Going on a Bear Hunt by Michael Rosen
The Cat in the Hat by Dr. Seuss
Alexander and the Terrible, Horrible, No Good Very Bad Day by Judith Viorst
Lyle, Lyle, Crocodile by Bernard Waber